TEACHING
THE DOG
TO **READ**

TEACHING
THE DOG
TO **READ**

Jonathan
Carroll

SUBTERRANEAN PRESS 2015

First Edition

ISBN
978-1-59606-725-7

Subterranean Press
PO Box 190106
Burton, MI 48519

subterraneanpress.com

for Alicja Krawiec
who fought the storm and won.
In celebration.

We don't remember the dream,
but the dream remembers us.
—Linda Pastan

he gift arrived in the regular mail: a nondescript square box wrapped in thick brown paper with a striking, quite beautiful royal blue and white mailing label on top saying it came from the Lichtenberg Watch Company.

Tony Areal's eyes widened on seeing that name because for the last few years one of his dreams was to own a Lichtenberg watch; in particular, the Lichtenberg 'Figure' wristwatch that cost over nine thousand dollars. He loved watches but most especially this one. However he had nowhere near the kind of money to spend on something as wonderfully frivolous and unnecessary as an almost ten grand wristwatch. It was a nice unrealistic dream, but one he returned to often. Whatever *was* in this package was probably some sort of nasty joke from a smartass friend who knew how much Areal coveted the beautiful timepiece. Whoever it was had somehow gotten hold of one of the Lichtenberg Company's mailing labels and stuck it on this box, hoping to trick Tony into believing his dream had magically come true and for once in his not-interesting-life the gods really *had* favored him for some mysterious reason. However on opening this surprising arrival of course he'd only find something dumb and disappointing inside, like a rubber duck or package of cheap condoms. Certainly not the glorious 'Figure' watch he had desired for so long.

He picked up his pocket knife and after opening it, carefully cut along one of the box's seams. He thought, "I know it isn't in here, but what the hell—until I see what *is*, I'm going to pretend it's a 'Figure.' For the next thirty seconds of my life I'm going to pretend some amazingly generous friend sent me a Lichtenberg watch out of the blue because they love me. Ha!"

He'd seen so many photos and video clips of the watch and the meticulous painstaking way it was made. He'd even watched with unwavering attention a YouTube clip of the "unboxing" of a 'Figure' (112 views) wherein some lucky guy who'd bought the watch filmed himself opening the simple but lovely cherrywood case with the signature two lightning bolts on the lid that was a 'Figure's' safe home when not being used.

TEACHING THE DOG TO READ

After opening all four flaps of the cardboard package and bending them backward, Areal pulled off a fat layer of protective plastic bubble wrap—and froze. Because there beneath it, he saw those instantly recognizable black lightning bolts...

"*What the hell...*" Mouth open in both awe and consternation, he awkwardly slid his hands down inside the cardboard and pulled out a square wooden box emblazoned with that oh-so familiar black logo on the lid. "*No way!*"

But it was real. He undid the small brass hook and eye holding the top closed (even that was beautifully made) and lifted it. Staring him right in the eye was a Lichtenberg 'Figure' watch addressed to the one and only Anthony Areal.

For a few moments he was almost, no he *was* afraid to take the watch out of the box. Maybe this was all a minutely detailed dream and the moment he actually *touched* the thing he'd either wake up in his real world where this treasure wasn't there inches in front of him, or it would turn into a pumpkin (or something else weird), like Cinderella's coach at midnight.

"Screw it!" Reaching down, he carefully tugged the heavy object out of the royal blue velvet that held it firmly in place. Even if this *was* a dream, once in his life Tony was going to actually hold a damned Lichtenberg 'Figure' watch in his hand.

And if it *were* real by some miracle, then the sooner that happened the better.

The watchband was a deep red oxblood color. He knew from reading on the Lichtenberg website that the leather was made by Horween, the best of the best. The watch's brushed aluminum case, black face with luminous white hands and numerals.... This *had* to be the real thing, although for a few mini seconds the paranoid thought flashed across his mind that it might only be a good copy of the watch, a hundred dollar knockoff made in some hellish sweatshop in Bangladesh, Bangalore, Belarus or worse. But the wooden box itself must have cost a lot, and the specific details everywhere like how the blue of the inner velvet exactly matched the blue on the mailing label...no, this had to be the real thing.

Heavy—the watch was so wonderfully heavy in his hand. It made him think of gold or some other precious metal that by weight alone tells you this shit is *real*; you are holding something *significant* in your hand, Son.

On his wrist he carefully adjusted the band to fit, then closed the wide metal clasp. It was gorgeous—better than he had ever imagined. The gratifying heaviness, the size, the faint erotic smell of new leather still on the band (he brought it to his nose to get a few good deep sniffs), the sheer

thereness of the watch on his, Tony Areal's, wrist…
He disliked and never used the by-now-exhausted
word 'awesome' because everybody else did 24/7,
but damn it this watch *was* awesome. There was no
other way to describe it.

He took a deep happy breath, stood and walked
across the room to a full length mirror mounted on
a wall there. For the next few minutes he preened
and posed in front of the long glass like a Milan
model, arm stiff out in front, wrist and watch
exposed to the mirror. Then watch hand on his
chin, his hip, his opposite shoulder, then stuffed
into his jeans pocket but not deep enough to hide
the silver beauty from the mirror's admiring eye….
Pose after different pose to see how his 'Figure'
looked in various set ups. Tony Areal was not a
vain man but if someone were to watch him in
front of the mirror for those minutes they would
have thought he was Narcissus loving his reflection
in the pool. He even tried a DeNiro impersonation
from *Taxi Driver*—"Are you talking to me?" He
wanted to see if the watch's magic gave him a little bit of Travis Bickle. It didn't and he knew his
imitation was awful, but what the hell—why not?
This timepiece could transform any Clark Kent
into Superman.

Tony was a happy man. He had the watch.
He had no idea *why* he had it or what great good

person in his life had given it to him, but for now he was content letting that mystery dangle from his mind like a key on a keychain. He walked back to the table and picked up the mailing box. Yes indeed, it was addressed to him—Anthony Areal—no mistake about that. Mr. Areal was now the proud owner of one Lichtenberg 'Figure' watch. The End.

A WEEK later it was the car. He worked in an office. He had a job. What he did at that job is not important. If I told you what it entailed you'd shrug, so let's skip Anthony Areal's professional bio and get right to the car. One day a bicycle messenger dressed all in yellow like a giant canary arrived in his office with a manila envelope for Tony. There was no return address on it which was sort of peculiar but sometimes it happened—a sender was in a hurry or simply forgot to put their address on.

When he opened it something fell out onto the floor—something metallic by the sound of it and heavy. Bending to pick it up, he saw it was a single fat key on a keychain. Both had the instantly recognizable gold, red and black logo of the Porsche automobile company on them.

TEACHING THE DOG TO READ

Tony frowned, straightened, and dropped the keychain on his desk. He stared at it a moment before picking up the envelope again and looking inside. There were quite a few pieces of different size and colored paper which on inspection turned out to be a car registration, certificate of ownership, an auto insurance policy paid in full and even a membership to the national auto club—all in the name of Anthony Areal.

The last piece of paper had a neat handwritten note on it. "The car is in the parking lot. The gas tank is full. This is the license plate number. Of course it's a gray metallic Cayman with coral red interior." Almost instinctively after reading the note he glanced down at the new watch on his wrist. It felt like he needed to confirm the exact time this was all happening to him even though he had no idea *what* was happening to him.

His sassy work colleague Lena Schabort walked by. Seeing the key on the desk, she stopped and put her hands on her hips. "Driving a Porsche these days, Tony?" The mocking derisive tone of her smoky voice said if *you* are driving a Porsche these days, then alligators can whistle Beethoven.

Like most men in the office, Tony had lusted after Lena ever since she came to work there, but knew he stood little chance. She was the kind of woman who only dated men who actually owned a

Porsche (or two) and had their shoes custom made in London. He most certainly did not. Lena was so bold and sure of herself that now she leaned over to his desk and without asking permission, read the handwritten note that had come with the key. A thin fog of doubt moved in over her eyes and she frowned. Had the world as she perceived it suddenly and rudely shifted a bit to the left? She stared coldly at Areal as if he had been deceiving her all along. Then she marched over to a large picture window that looked out on the company parking lot. It took maybe ten seconds for her to scan the lot and locate the car. "*Come here,*" she commanded. Her back was turned but plainly she meant Tony.

Right then a strange thing happened: he didn't move. He didn't do what she ordered which ten minutes ago would have been unthinkable. Ten minutes ago he would have gotten Lena Schabort fried clams from Florida if she'd asked. But now he didn't move. Even more interesting is he didn't *need* to move because he knew—he knew he knew he knew—that the car was *there.* Down in the parking lot waiting for him, zero mileage, was a brand new gunmetal gray Porsche Cayman with coral red leather interior registered in his name—the car of his dreams. He knew.

"Tony? Is *that* your car down there?" She was pointing out the window.

"Yes." He still didn't move.

"When did you get it?"

He gave his best Robert DeNiro one shoulder, *Good Fellas* no-big-deal shrug. "Ah, recently."

Lena turned from the window and looked at him a long time without saying anything. A beautiful new Porsche. Tony Areal. What else didn't she know about this man?

Frank Rothner from billing came down the corridor and sidled over to Lena. He was so predictable—the whole office knew he used any excuse to get close to her. "What's up?"

"Did you know that Tony drives a Porsche?"

Rothner grinned like a lottery winner. He'd recently spent a fortune getting his teeth straightened and whitened, so he smiled whenever he could. Plus he thought Lena was joking and wanted her to know that no one in the world appreciated her sense of humor more than him. He looked at Tony dismissively, as if he were the butt of a joke. When he spoke his voice wore ten pounds of sarcasm, "*Really,* a Porsche? What model, pal?"

Tony stood up from his chair. He looked at the floor and smiled to himself a happy moment, putting off the gratifying *coup de grace* he knew was imminent. Vengeance really *is* a dish best tasted cold. He took out the certificate of ownership and walked over to Rothner with it in hand. "A Cayman

GTS, *Pal*. Three hundred and forty horsepower with every option you can imagine *and* a custom red leather interior." Handing Frank the certificate, Tony stood with one hand in his pocket while the other man scanned it.

Doubt and then...waiiiit for it...yup—a delicious little frisson of *outrage* showed on Rothner's face as the fact of what Tony had said sank in. Blinking too much, he did not do a good job of hiding that rage when returning the paper.

"That's pretty, uh..." Stumped, Frank looked at Lena as if she knew what word he should say now. "That's awesome, man. I had no idea." Frank always made fun of Tony. How many times had he said different variations of sentences like, "Hey gang, it's A-real-Tony in our midst!" Lame word play like that, jibes and sometimes not so subtle verbal cattle prods, were annoying after the zillionth time. And it wasn't only that. Tony frequently had the feeling Frank Rothner didn't like him but there was no reason for it. The two men had almost no contact professionally or otherwise. About the only thing they had in common was their interest in Lena Schabort, not that she was interested in either of them.

"Who's the woman, Tony? Is that your girlfriend?"

"Huh?"

"In your car; there's a woman sitting in the passenger's seat. Who is she?" Lena's voice was now wheedling and thin, as if she was trying to coax/flirt the answer out of him. In the world according to Lena S, anyone who owned an eighty thousand dollar car had backbone and didn't answer any questions they didn't want to. In her estimation, Tony Areal's backbone had miraculously transformed from a wet noodle to a titanium rod in the last ten minutes.

"What are you talking about?" Tony strode to the window and looked out. He paid no attention to the fact he was now standing closer to Lena Schabort than he had in all the time he'd known her. But to him at that moment she might as well have been a Coke machine.

The first hard thump in his heart came when looking out the window, he located the gleaming gunmetal gray German machine down in the lot for the first time. There it was—his car, *his* Porsche. The papers to prove it were right here in his hand. Hot damn!

The second heart thump came on seeing the elbow, arm and the long hair. A woman *was* sitting in the passenger's seat of his car. Her window was down and a thin bare arm and elbow rested comfortably on the door there. She must have had long hair because even that was visible from this distance too.

"Who is she?"

"I have *no* idea." Tony turned to Lena wearing a smile that until an hour ago he didn't possess. It was the devilish, confident, everything's-coming-up-roses smile successful people throw at the world when they know success or at least something interesting is right around the corner for them—again. The arrogant self assured smile of people used to having nice things happen to them often. Tony turned away from his long time object of desire and headed for the door.

Sensing opportunity, Frank sidled up to Lena again and said indignantly, "What the hell's gotten into him?"

Lena looked at Rothner like he was a contagious disease. "Why do you always have to stand so close to me, Frank? Are you some kind of perv?"

Before Frank could say anything in his own defense, she shook her head in disgust and strode off.

When he was sure she was far enough away, Frank lifted his chin and sniffed the air. The sillage of Lena's perfume still hung there, as it always deliciously did after she'd made an exit. Savoring it, he realized he was sniffing too much and his eyes were closed as he did it. Snapping to open-eyed attention, he looked around to make sure no one had seen him perv'ing the air like that. Then he hurried back to his desk.

TEACHING THE DOG TO READ

TONY AREAL pushed open the door and stepped outside. It was a beautiful day—sunny but cool enough to wear a light jacket. His favorite kind of weather. He held the envelope containing all the car documents in case the mysterious woman in the Porsche was somehow officially connected to this. As he got closer to the car he saw more of her in silhouette. She did have long, what appeared to be auburn hair and wore large sunglasses that concealed much of her upper face. Sensing his approach, she turned slowly to him and slipped the glasses down her nose but not off. She was okay looking but that wasn't what caused him to make a sudden stutter step.

He *recognized* her. He didn't know when or where he'd seen the woman before but she definitely occupied a piece of real estate in his memory.

Auburn hair, pale skin, a small mouth, and brown eyes that looked amused but non-committal. "*There* you are. I've been waiting." Her voice was high pitched and friendly. It sounded familiar too. Where the hell had he seen this woman before?

Tony stood a few feet from the car, waiting for her to say something else, to explain her presence here. But she said nothing so they watched each other in silence.

"Are we having a staring contest?"

His mouth twitched into a smile. "Do we *know* each other? You look familiar."

"Why don't you join me for lunch and we'll talk about it." She reached down to her feet and brought up a large white bag. "I brought sandwiches. And root beer."

That startled him. Root beer was his favorite drink when he was a boy and even into adulthood Tony always kept a can or two in his refrigerator. How did she know he liked it?

"Come on, let's go. I'm dying to ride in this beautiful car." She waved for him to get in.

Tony lowered himself into the driver's seat and gently put his open hands at ten and two o'clock on the steering wheel. Overcome by the moment, he took them off again and rubbed his face. "I can't believe this."

The woman gathered her hair back into a ponytail and quickly wrapped a rubber band around it.

Dropping his right hand down to the shift lever, for the first time he saw something there that gave him pause. "It's automatic."

"What is?"

"The car—it's an automatic."

"Yes, so what?"

Frowning, he bit his lip. "I don't know. My Porsche—the one I always wanted—had a six speed. It was a manual transmission."

TEACHING THE DOG TO READ

Areal was looking at the shifter in his hand while speaking so he didn't see her expression darken and then quickly change right back to neutral.

"Is that a problem?"

"No, of course not. I thought—"

"What did you think, Tony?"

Hearing her speak his name swung his attention. "How do you know me? Where have we met? *What are you doing here?*"

She ignored the question and pointed to his left wrist instead. "Nice watch."

Disconcerted, he looked at her and then at his watch. Her again, the watch again. "You know about this?"

"Sure, your own Lichtenberg 'Figure.' A Porsche and a Lichtenberg watch—hand in hand. Oh come on Tony, didn't you think for even a minute that there *might* be a connection between them—the two things you've been coveting forever suddenly appear out of the blue? Now they're yours, one right after the other.

"*Plus* a root beer for lunch! What more could Señor Areal want?" She reached into the bag, brought out a bottle of the soda and unscrewed the plastic top. "Want some?"

He shook his head slowly.

She took a swig and wiped her top lip. "I'll give you a hint, but only one: Tuna Fish."

"*Tuna fish?*"

"Yup—tuna fish." She drank again.

"That's not much help."

She pointed the root beer bottle at his head. "Then dig deeper. The answer is right in there, I promise you."

He put the key in the ignition and started the engine. "Where should we go?"

She said, "I don't care—surprise me. No, no wait a minute—drive to the river. Let's have our lunch by the water."

Neither of them said anything during the drive from Tony's office to the river. Down there a short distance from the parking lot were some green metal picnic tables close by the water. Several were occupied, including one with a bunch of loud teenage boys horsing around and showing off for each other. They all went quiet and stared as Tony and the woman walked by them to the table farthest away. Making sure his friends were watching and that the woman had her back completely turned to him, one boy licked his lips like a starving slobbering wolf in a cartoon and stretching out both arms, pretended to reach for her ass with both hands after she'd passed him.

When his friends erupted in a chorus of snorts and sniggers, the woman stopped; half turning, she said over her shoulder, "Dream on, Marcus—You'll never score an ass as good as mine."

Hoots! Howls! One of the boys laughed so hard he fell off the table which brought on another wave of shrieks.

Marcus was horrified—how could she possibly have seen what he did when he was certain her back was to him? And how did she know his name?

"Hey man, you *know* her?"

"N-no. I've never seen her before."

"Yeah well then how did she know your name, bro?"

"I... I don't know."

This Marcus must have been the leader of that crew because by the time Tony Areal and the woman had reached their table, the boys were quietly leaving but not before most of them cast backward glances at this chick who'd jammed up their boy good.

Sitting down at the table, she opened the bag and took out two sandwiches wrapped in wax paper. She undid one and slid it on its paper across the table for Tony. He hadn't sat down yet—just stood tensely facing her on the other side of the table, sizing this all up in his head. "You knew that kid?"

"No. Come on, eat your sandwich." She took the two bottles of root beer out of the bag and put them on the table. "Eat something. We'll talk in a minute. It'll make you think better." Holding her sandwich in two hands, she took a big bite and hummed to let him know how tasty it was.

He didn't sit but not having eaten anything that day, he was hungry. Picking up the fat sandwich, he saw it was one of his favorites—pastrami on rye bread with coleslaw and Russian dressing. At that moment he didn't even feel it necessary to ask her how she knew. He took a big bite because he couldn't think of what he wanted to say to her although there were so many questions going through his head.

As he took another bite and chewed, he watched a lovely tall woman walking a Hungarian Vizsla dog near the river's edge. The dog was not on a line but stayed close to the woman, constantly looking up at her as if to make sure she didn't stray too far.

Boom! It hit Tony and he froze in mid-chew. Tuna. The dog. A dog named Tuna. The dream. *That* dream.

Great sleep dreams seduce and sometimes torture. The best ones can almost break our heart when we awaken from them and find ourselves back…here. I'm talking about those exceedingly rare dreams we've all had over the course of our lives *so* splendid or sexy or momentous or idyllic or all of those things *combined* that we never want them to end and are genuinely distraught on waking and those luminous experiences and images immediately begin to vanish into our never-very-trustworthy memory. No romantic moments in waking life have been greater than those in that one walk-in-the-forest dream you had when you were 19; the dream with the 101% perfect mate who faded away like morning mist as soon as you came awake. Or the magnificent candlelight meal outside under the trees in the garden of that small French *auberge* where both the mood and meal tasted like the gods had prepared them only for you. And remember the bliss you felt on meeting your dead parent (brother, sister, best friend…) in some unimportant place—an empty parking lot or a small rural airport. You sat together like in the old days and spoke about things that brought you peace and a heart-filling reminder of the strength of the love that lost person once had for you when they were alive.

Tony Areal once dreamt of a dog named Tuna. In this dream which ended up being epic, he was sitting at a bus stop by the sea (who knows where?). The weather was summer-beautiful. He was content to sit on the bench and wait for a bus while watching the waves come and go a short distance away across the road. The warmth of the day, the smell of brine and hot asphalt, and the beautiful monotony of the tumbling sea had lulled him into a kind of half-hypnotic trance. His whole countenance drooped contentedly and he felt like he was stoned.

What a shock when suddenly something big and twisty banged hard into his right leg and then squirmed up against it. Snapping out of his stupor, he looked down and saw a large brown and black mixed breed dog at his feet looking up at him with joyful friendly eyes and a long pink tongue lolling out the side of its mouth.

Tony liked dogs and had no fear of them. "Hello there, guy. What's your name?" Reaching down, he stroked the big beast under the chin. Its eyes immediately half closed in pleasure.

"His name is Tuna."

Tony looked up to his right and saw a tall pretty woman in denim shorts, a white tee shirt and a cloth backpack. She wore a half battered and bent Panama straw hat tipped jauntily to one side and leather flip flop sandals so worn down and ratty that they looked like they'd been around the world a few times on heavy feet. Taking all of her in with one long look, he saw this woman really *did* have large feet.

"His name is Tuna and yes, I really do have big feet."

Tony didn't know what to say. He was embarrassed and curious in equal measure. Who names a dog Tuna and how the hell did she know what he thought about her feet?

TEACHING THE DOG TO READ

"I'm teaching him how to read." She said this as if it were no big deal.

"You're teaching a dog to *read*?"

"That's right." She sat down on the bench next to a now-slightly bewildered Anthony Areal and crossing her bare legs, took hold of one knee with both hands. Her fingers were long and thin, the nails short and unpainted. Her dog leaned against Tony's leg, pawing him gently to continue each time the man stopped petting it.

"How *do* you teach a dog to read?"

"Start by teaching them the alphabet."

For some reason her logical answer spoken in a matter-of-fact voice struck Tony as funny and he chuckled.

"Do you have a better way?" She asked, sounding eager to know.

He threw up his hands as if surrendering to the police. "No, not at all. I didn't even know you *could* do that."

She shrugged. "Tuna looks bored a lot if we're not outside or actually doing something. If he could read, I think it would make his life nicer."

The lovely lunacy of that thought and the image of a dog reading a newspaper made Tony grin again.

They talked about this and that until a small silver and red bus pulled up and stopped in front of them. The door hissed opened and the driver looked to see if they wanted to get on. They looked at each other and that one silent glance settled it—Tony raised a hand and smiling, waved a 'no thanks' to the driver—they were staying here. The bus drove off and the most sublime day Tony Areal ever spent with a woman began.

After a while they stood and walked across the hot pavement to the beach. While Tuna raced around chasing indignant seagulls and anything else the dog found interesting, Tony and the woman—only after some time did she tell him her name was Alice—talked. Talked and talked and talked. She was smart and wickedly funny, insightful and observant in a way that straight away had him eager to hear anything she had to say about whatever topic they were discussing. It was like that the whole afternoon. It kept getting better and better but never once did they touch—only talked and laughed and learned how the other saw the world around them.

"That was me."

"What?"

The woman sitting across the picnic table at the river took a bite of her sandwich and chewed. She held up a finger for Tony to wait till she'd swallowed.

"I was Alice that day, that woman in your dream. Do you remember how it ended?"

TEACHING THE DOG TO READ

"No." He only remembered how marvelous it had been spending time with Alice who wanted to teach her dog to read.

The mysterious woman put her sandwich down and wiped her lips with a paper napkin. "We went back to the bus stop. It was getting dark by then and I said I had to go. When the bus pulled up, I gave you one of those," she pointed to his Lichtenberg. "It was in my backpack the whole time."

Tony looked hard at the watch on his wrist. "I don't remember any of that; only how we walked on the beach and talked the whole time while the dog ran around."

"Well, that's what happened." The mysterious woman nodded twice as if to affirm what she'd said.

"So you're Alice, the woman from my dream?"

"No, not quite." She pulled a piece of bread off her sandwich and flipped it to three pigeons waddling around near their feet.

Tony shook his head. "But you said—"

The woman tore off another piece of bread and dropped it for the birds. "Do you remember what Alice looked like?"

Tony hesitated a moment, thinking. "No, not really. She was pretty but not gorgeous or anything."

The woman turned away from him so that her face was hidden, then seconds later turned back.

She had a completely different face. "Did she look like this?'

Shocked, Tony gasped. He needed time to even barely shake his head no. "I…don't know, I don't remember. What have you—"

Holding up a hand to stop him talking, again the woman did the 'turn away/turn back' thing. This time she had a completely *different* face, that of a stunningly beautiful Eurasian with long licorice-shiny hair falling down her back like a black waterfall. Tony gaped slack jawed, eyes wide with disbelief and fear.

"Do you remember *her*?"

"No."

"Oh Tony—where's your memory? Here's a last one." A third time she pivoted away and then back wearing yet a third new face—a California blond this time—big sensual mouth, cornflower blue eyes, white-blond hair. A surfer girl deluxe.

"I don't understand. What are you *doing*? I-I can't do this… I'm going to go now." Shaken to the marrow of his bones, Tony was barely able to stand up from the table.

"Sit down. I'm not finished."

He remained standing, ready to bolt.

"*Sit down.*" The woman said threateningly. If her voice had been a gun, it would have been cocked and pointed an inch from his eye.

He sat.

"Those are all faces *you* created, Tony. Those three women and thousands of others you first saw and then borrowed from your life. Or you fashioned them entirely out of your imagination for the 13,487 dreams you've had in your 37 years."

"Thirteen thousand *what*?"

"Night dreams—that's how many you've had in your life. Or I should say *we've* had."

Silence. After waiting a while for Tony to say something, the woman took another big bite of sandwich and chewed with one eye closed while watching him intently with the other, a hint of a smile on her moving lips. He did nothing but stare at her. Only once did he lick his lips because his mouth had gone as dry as a lizard.

"Who *are* you?"

She nodded. *Finally* he was asking. It was about time! "Who? I'm *you*, but the night shift version Tony."

"What do you mean?"

She finished the sandwich and patted her thin mouth with a green paper napkin. "I could have come here today looking exactly like you, Tony. You saw what I'm capable of doing. But I didn't want to freak you out, so I'm here as some woman you walked past in one of your dreams a decade ago; no one important or in any way memorable.

"I thought it best to break all of this to you gently and slowly, one step at a time. So first I sent you the watch a few weeks ago, then the Porsche today. Now this nice lunch together with your favorite sandwiches, the two of us..."

Unconsciously Tony touched his wrist. "It was *you* who gave me this?"

"Sure, who else do you know who'd give you a nine grand watch? You've had it in so many of your dreams lately that I thought you'd like to have one of your own. Do you like it?"

Areal stared down at his wrist and frowned stupidly, as if he had been smacked on the head and was dazed by the blow. In a dead monotone he said, "Yes. It's nice."

She puffed out her lips and said sarcastically, "*Nice*? That's it? Your dream comes true and all you can say is 'it's nice'?"

Tony undid the watch and put it on the table in front of her. "Take it. I don't want it anymore."

She slid it back across the table towards him. "No, that's okay—you can keep it; the Porsche too if you like. It's only stuff. We've got much more important matters to discuss."

TEACHING THE DOG TO READ

WHEN HE returned to work that afternoon, Anthony Areal was a changed man. Lena Schabort noticed it first. Tony strode into the office like a guy who'd won two lotteries and a date with Miss Brazil. Seeing pretty Lena, he pointed his thumb and index finger at her like a gun and gave her the coolest, sexiest wink she'd ever seen. It absolutely stunned her—one wink—Wham! If someone had asked her to describe *why* it was so special she wouldn't have known what to say. But its effect continued to slide slow and sensuously like a bead of sex-sweat down the exact middle of her flat tummy and *stayed*.

She happened to be talking to Rick "The Prick" Olivier when Tony passed and Rick was the first to comment about the noticeable difference in his work colleague. That in itself was surprising because Olivier had an ego the size of Switzerland. He rarely noticed or expressed interest in anything other than his own reflection in the world around him. In fact at the moment Tony appeared, Olivier was yet again trying to coax Lena into a date but with little success. He stopped in mid-pitch when Areal swept confidently by them after that quick devastating wink at her.

Rick scoffed. "What's with Areal? He looks like he's high."

Lena snorted disgustedly. "No Dear, he looks like he's *hot. Damn*."

The Prick didn't like hearing that and tried to steer the conversation back to him. "So what do you say Lena, you wanna go out or what?"

"Rick, I'd rather have eye surgery in a *helicopter* than go out with you." She flashed him a huge fake smile that lasted two seconds before striding off towards Areal's desk. It was the long way around to her own but she *had* to get a second helping of the man to see if what she'd experienced of him was as hotwired as it felt.

"ALOHA!"

Tony was scowling at a paper in his hand when he heard this. Looking up, he saw the very attractive brown haired woman he'd passed in the hall looking at him, a little wild eyed because she seemed sort of over-excited about something. It was why Lena had greeted him with that ridiculous, out of nowhere, trying-to-be-cute-and-amusing-at-the-same-time word. But while continuing to smile maniacally at him, she was thinking '<u>Aloha</u>? *It's so dumb*. Why did I have to say *that*?' Suddenly she felt as awkward as a fifteen year old sophomore talking to the most popular senior class boy in high school. At the same time, she thought *Tony Areal? I've got my panties and head in a twist about him?*

Tony had to think a bit before he recognized her. "Lena? Lena Schabort?"

She tried to giggle but it sort of stuck in her throat. "Uh yeah, Tony, don't you recognize me?" Her voice was half tease, half scold with a little desperation in there too. She thought he was teasing her because she knew he had the hots for her, like most of the other men in the office.

"I do indeed recognize you, Ms. Lena. Weren't you my wife in our last life?"

The line was so saucy, sweet and unexpected especially coming from him that her mouth fell open in surprise. She quickly put a hand over it while staring at this fellow who looked exactly like he had an hour ago but now somehow seemed an entirely different person.

"Did something happen, Tony? I mean, are you okay?"

He smiled and tilted his head a little to the side as if to indicate he didn't understand why she asked. "*Happen?* No, nothing happened. Why?"

"Because you seem really different; like, *completely* different than you were when we talked an hour ago. You know, right before you went down to your new car in the parking lot. I saw you talking to that woman inside it and when you two drove away I thought something might have happened. Maybe something she said?"

Tony shook his head. "Ah! No, the opposite—she was there to give me some good news, really good news. Maybe that's why I seem different now?"

That sounded logical to her. Each of them waited for the other to say more but nothing came. Lena realized she was staring at his mouth. She realized she was wondering what it would be like to kiss that mouth. She wondered if she was going nuts. "Tony?"

He was looking down again at the paper in his hand.

"Would you like to go for a drink after work today?"

He raised his eyes slowly. They were amused and he was smiling. "No."

Stunned, Lena was speechless a moment. She had never asked a man to go out. She had never been so blatantly rejected by one either. "Oh… well…uh sorry…"

He reached out and took her arm. "But I would *love* to go dancing with you. Could we do that instead?"

She lit up like a 4th of July sparkler because she loved to dance. It was her great passion and the office knew it. "Really, you dance? What kind… what's your favorite?"

He pointed his index finger at her, "It's up to you—I'm game for anything, Ginger Rogers."

In a small hopeful voice she asked hesitantly, "Do you tango?"

Tony Areal jumped up, grabbed Lena Schabort around the waist, and taking her right hand in his left, extended both arms out stiffly to the side in the classic tango pose. Face close enough to hers so she could feel his warm breath on her cheek, he said in a voice sexy enough to seduce a nun, "Nope, not a step. But you can teach me."

THE TWO Tonys sat on the same bus stop bench by the sea, comparing notes. Tony Night Shift lit a cigarette.

Tony Day didn't smoke and scowled when he smelled it. "So how did it go for you?"

Tony Night sighed. "—was okay. We went out, went dancing, had something to eat, then went back to her place. Afterwards I came home, went to sleep and *voila* here I am, dreaming. End of story."

"Did you do it with Lena?"

"Yeah." Tony Night shrugged again. After dragging deeply on the cig he let out a thick white plume of smoke. Two cars passed by going in opposite directions.

"And?"

"And *what*?" Another long pull on the cigarette.

Tony Day slapped his forehead in frustration. "How was it? How was *she*?"

"Dull, Dude, dull. She looks all sexy and delicious on the outside, right? But in the sack she hardly moves, never does anything interesting or original, and doesn't make a sound. You might as well take yourself out on a date. You'd have better sex at the end of the night."

Tony Day couldn't help grinning. So Foxy Lena was all show and no go, eh? In contrast he'd come from the exact opposite experience with the lovely, bewitching, sexy-as-all-hell Alice. What a day it had been with her!

Tony Night saw that contentment and said sourly, "I take it from the happy look on *your* face that things went well with Alice?"

Tony Day sighed with pleasure. "They did. Hands down it was the best time I've *ever* had with a woman."

Tony Night said in a monotone, "Glad to hear it."

"You don't sound glad."

"Well Brother I'm actually not, truth be told. I had a shit time while you had a great one. It wasn't supposed to go that way, you know? *Both* of us were supposed to benefit from this swap of ours. But here you are beaming like a flashlight and I just had sex with a mop."

Tony Day grinned. "A *mop*?"

TEACHING THE DOG TO READ

"You know what I mean."

"Hey, *you* were the one who wanted to do this. *You* came to me and said let's switch jobs for a while: You take the day shift and I'll take the night. We're doing what you wanted."

Tony Night nodded while grinding out the cigarette but he didn't say anything.

"So?"

"So *what*?"

Tony Day asked, "Is our deal still on or do you want your job back? I've got to say, so far I love being the Tony who lives in and controls his night dreams." He stretched both arms out wide to the sides. "I get to create my own *world* here night after night. It's amazing! Live out all the dreams and fantasies I've ever had? Yes please. Bring Alice back whenever I want for another fabulous time with her. Or I could have a movie star, like Arlen Ford…

"Hey, what do you think of my new car?" Parked down the road from the bus stop was a brand new white Aston Martin 'Vanquish,' the Oz of automobiles in Tony Areal's universe. Now, *here*, he had one. The keys were in his pocket.

Tony Night briefly glanced at it and smirked. "No more lowly Porsches for *you*, huh? Well it's certainly jazzy— Childish, but that's okay. We all want to play with the toys when they're new. After a while though stuff like that won't spark your noodle anymore, believe me."

A loud ominous rumbling sound came from down the road. Both men turned toward it. A bunch of rhinoceros and bull terrier dogs came thundering towards them. The much smaller dogs ran right beside and among the huge galloping beasts as if they were all comrades in arms charging into battle. The air suddenly reeked of mud and heavy animal musk, wood smoke, dung, rotten fruit and unknown wholly exotic smells. It was as if the stench and perfume of wildest Africa had arrived all at once.

Tony Day's eyes grew enormous and he made to scramble the hell off the bench and away. But the other Tony grabbed his arm and shaking his head, held him there.

"It's okay, we're safe."

Tony Day looked alarmed but didn't move. The rhinos and dogs reached them quickly but without pause pounded past as if all were racing flat out towards some invisible finish line far off in the distance. Thirteen, fourteen, fifteen of the magnificent monsters raced down the road next to the sea, accompanied by no telling how many of Tony Day's favorite dogs. When in his life had he seen anything like *this*?

As soon as the stampede had passed he sang out ecstatically, "That was *amazing*! I love them both so much—but rhinos and bull terriers running *together*? Those are my two absolute favorite animals. Do you know a group of rhinos is called a 'crash'?"

This did not interest Tony Night. "You'll get used to that kind of nutty scene the longer you're here. This is Anthony Areal Dreamland, remember—the ultimate mixed salad of everything you are, all whizzed up together in weird combinations and presented in nightly servings. Don't be surprised to see a *lot* of what you like or know here. Favorite dogs, old friends *and* enemies—they're all here. Sometimes it'll come straight as fact, other times squashed and smooshed together, like in any dream." He pointed down the road towards where the animals had gone. "And to tell the truth, it's not always pleasant or cool like that little stampede of your favorites. But all that's here came from *your* life, good and bad. Rhinos, your favorite cars, even Mrs. Zlabinger is somewhere. I saw her the other day playing a trombone."

"My eleventh grade English teacher?"

"Yup. Don't be surprised if you bump into her and she asks if you've finished your Shakespeare essay yet. Welcome to Tony Dreamland, Mr. Areal. You are the sole creator and proprietor now."

Tony Day considered all this while out of the corner of his eye he saw his exquisite new automobile parked down the road. He couldn't wait to drive it again. "But what about you? I've got to say truthfully that compared to what goes on here, my old life is a big bore."

Tony Night shook his head. "And that's absolutely *fine* with me. I needed a change, man. I had to get out of here and live some *normal*, you know? No rhinos suddenly running down the road or other weird crap. Good old plain donuts and black coffee for breakfast for me, thanks. When you've lived at the circus all your life, it's great to take a break from the clowns and zebras, you know? For me after being here all these years, it's a real pleasure being bored for a while."

That answer made sense to Tony Day but he still was puzzled about something. "If I *am* in charge of things here, and I arrange the ingredients of your dreams, why that stampede now? I didn't order it. Alice and the car yes, but not that." He pointed down the road.

Tony Night took a deep breath, knowing he was going to have to do some explaining now. "Think of it this way: when you were living where I am now, you passed your days constantly experiencing this great huge *mass* of various things. Whether you were aware of it or not, most of that stuff went into your memory and *stayed*: The ugly woman with the green purse at the Mexican restaurant, that long distance phone call with your funny sister…

"It's like you'd go to the market every day and buy bags and bags full of groceries. But there was no logic to what you put in them. Eventually you'd bring all those bags home and give them to me, Tony Night. I'd sift through what you'd brought and choose which ones I wanted to cook. Then I'd combine them together into your nightly dream.

"But sometimes life or fate interferes. You forget to buy the tomatoes but you don't feel like going back to the store to get them. So the meal is cooked without tomatoes. The same with my job—sometimes things get added or subtracted from the dreams because of, I don't know, outside sources or forces or whatever you want to call it. Hey look—you're never in complete control of either your life or your dreams. You love rhinos and bull terriers. For some reason they decided to make a guest appearance together in *this* dream. No reason why they showed up. But it was cool, right? So enjoy it."

IT'S NOT hard to guess which Tony was lying. Lena Schabort was sensational in bed—ravenous, endlessly inventive, and almost overwhelming in her horizontal skills. But Tony Night was not about to tell his counterpart *that*. Hell no. If he did, what if Tony Day said he wanted to sleep with her too? Worse, what if he said I don't want to do this switch anymore? I want to go back to who I was.

On the other hand from the sound of it, there wasn't much reason to worry. Tony Day was smitten with the sheer novelty and power of running Dreamland where it was true—he *could* create any dream he wanted to show each night on the big screen TV inside the other Tony's head.

In his first few attempts, the dreams he created were pretty tentative and as dull as a documentary about fish hatcheries in Finland. In one he sat in his boyhood kitchen watching his Mom make an egg soufflé while a bright orange SONY radio on the counter played pop hits from his childhood. Limahl's song "The Neverending Story" almost had him in tears because it was so packed with happy memories. In another dream, Tony and his sister ran around a lush meadow in a driving summer rainstorm in their underwear, heads bent back, mouths wide open to catch raindrops on their tongues, arms out to either side as if they were flying. The only odd thing about it was in the dream they were adults, not little kids. And *that* detail, like the racing rhinoceros, was not his doing.

It wasn't until the eleventh dream that Tony Day returned to the bus stop by the sea and a meeting with the wonderful Alice. Why wait so long? Simply because he was afraid he might do it wrong and spoil everything. The dream where they first met had been so perfect (as far as he remembered) that if he were to continue it now, he wanted to make sure he was totally in control of what he was doing. Hell, he'd wanted to meet up with Alice the first time he created a dream in his new role but his wiser self said no, wait long enough to figure out how to do this dreammaking right.

The ingredients at his disposal were his life. The goal? To use some of them to create the perfect setting and circumstances for a second meeting with this woman who appeared to embody everything he loved. But where should that meeting take place, and what should the circumstances be? Some romantic spot in Europe perhaps—a seaside *taverna* on a remote Greek island, or a 19th century mountaintop hotel in Switzerland with a panoramic view of the Eiger or Matterhorn? Tony Day had been to places like these in real life. Their majesty and beauty wrote their signatures on his soul, but were they the right backdrop for this meeting with Alice? Eventually he decided no because he didn't want the 'frame' to be more beautiful or interesting than a picture that had yet to be painted. Plus, what if she spent the whole time they were together staring at the surroundings and paid little attention to him?

He knew it was possible to create any dream right down to the smallest most insignificant detail. If he wanted, he could even script exactly what Alice would say and do when they met, but what would be the point of that? If he knew what the outcome would be, why even create the dream at all? Best to set the scene, then step back and let things take their course.

Is it a treasure or torment to have every single past moment of your life at your disposal when creating the ultimate romantic dream? The heavenly smells of cinnamon, oranges or cloves, the unexpected smile of a stranger, the paralyzing cold of a mountain stream on hot bare July skin, the whistle of a distant train, the sky ballet of a flock of birds… Millions, *billions*, of things, details, memories, mind-photos…to sift through and then choose only a few to create the landscape and mood Tony Day wanted to wrap around this Alice when they met again.

"But you ended up back *here* on this fucked up bench in the middle of nowhere. How'd *that* happen?" Tony Night asked, genuinely interested. "With all that material to choose from, you decided *this* was the best place to rendezvous with her? You are a strange fellow." He took out of his pocket and lit up one of those awful little Indian *beedi* cigarettes that smell like burnt pocket lint.

TEACHING THE DOG TO READ

"When did you start smoking *those*?" Tony Day said disdainfully when they met for only the second time.

"Today. Someone in the office offered one to me and I kind of liked it, so I bought a pack."

"Those things are horrible! Smoking's bad enough, but now you're into *them*?"

Tony Night took a puff and waved his hand for the other to continue his story. "So why *did* you want to meet Miss Perfect here again? You obviously weren't trying to impress her."

Ashamed, Tony Day looked at his feet and rubbed his knees. He wanted to say one thing but knew it was a lie, and on this subject he didn't want to lie. "Fear, I guess. Plain old fear."

Tony Night barked a loud laugh and shook his head ruefully. "Shit! I know exactly what you mean. You didn't want to make a mistake with her, right? So you opted for something that had already worked once. When in doubt, play it safe. God, you and I are such cowards! I totally understand why you did it." He chuckled again and took another hit off the stinky cigarette. "But then again, it *was* a pretty great dream, I have to admit."

Tony Day straightened up and rubbed his knees again. "You think so? I'm glad. I didn't know how you'd react."

Tony Night nodded. "Personally I like a rendez-vous that's more down and dirty. Like those dreams you had about Lena a while ago? *Those* were hot stuff. But hey, you're in charge of this department now and I'm only here to deliver the raw material.

"Anyway, I thought your dream was very Zen, stripped down and basic but in the best way. You guys met here, walked on the beach with the dog again and ate burgers: simple and sweet.

"But you know what part I liked best? How at the end of the meal she reached over and took that last French fry off your plate. That's a *very* intimate gesture. You gotta have something good going with another person to feel free to take their last fry."

Tony Day grinned. "Yes, wasn't that cool!"

"It was. You didn't make it happen?"

"Nope. The whole dream was unscripted; that was the best part. Only where I drove up in the Aston and she and Tuna were already waiting here—I made *that* up. But afterwards it was all free style."

"Then hat-tip to you, Brother. I think she's hooked. Wait a minute—do you hear something?"

An unfamiliar rumbling came from far down the road. The two men looked at each other and shook their heads simultaneously—neither knew what was happening and certainly hadn't summoned whatever was coming their way.

TEACHING THE DOG TO READ

The noise grew but oddly nothing appeared.

Tony Night finally asked, "Is this something you cooked up?"

"No, I have no idea what it is."

Louder and louder until the colossal sound felt like it was right on top of them but still they saw nothing.

Then as quickly the noise subsided—much faster than it did the time the rhinos and bull terriers raced by them.

Tony Night slapped his forehead. "Ah, I know what that was—the *ants*. How could I forget? Jeez, I live in your world only a few weeks and already I'm forgetting things."

"*What* ants? What are you talking about?"

"The ants in big shoes."

Tony Day stared blankly at the other man, completely lost.

"You don't remember?"

"Remember *what*?"

"Your ant nightmares."

Another *huh*? look from Tony Day.

"*Really*, you don't remember? Wow, that's incredible. When we were a boy you saw an old black and white cartoon about a picnic overrun by ants. I thought it was funny and harmless, but for some reason you latched onto the idea and many of the worst nightmares of our whole childhood were centered around ants wearing big shoes kidnapping you and taking you prisoner inside an anthill as big as a Disneyland ride."

"No way! I don't remember any of that."

"It's the truth, Buddy: You were scared shitless of a bunch of ants wearing brown wingtip shoes on their feet. I thought it was only a dopey cartoon, but you sure didn't; you used to wake up screaming and brushing your arms crazily like they were climbing all over you." Tony Night pointed to the empty road in front of them. "Ergo I think we witnessed the return of the biggest boogey men of our youth—ants in big shoes. Welcome back to Tony Dreamland."

THE REAL trouble began when both men fell in love. In one case it was entirely predictable, but in the other not so. Much to his surprise, Lena Schabort made Tony Night a better man. That sounds like an old bromide but in this case it was true. Almost more interesting was the fact he made Lena a better woman.

It began with the sex, which was fireworks between them from the start and more than enough to make Tony Night happy and content. Lena seemed happy too and for those first few weeks they spent most of their time together in bed.

But one day at work she walked by his desk and dropped a note on it. He was surprised to see she didn't stop to watch while he read it as she'd done before when her first note to him at the office said, "I want your tongue in my mouth right now." This time she almost flung her second note onto his desk and hurried away without even glancing at him. He thought that was sort of odd, but Lena had her own way of doing things and so far he was okay with it.

Unlike the first note which had been carefully folded in two, this piece of paper was crumpled up into a tight ball like something to throw away. Only later did he learn Lena almost *did* throw the note away because she was afraid of how he would react to its message. That explained the crumple.

"Thank you for last night. It was tender and wild and beautiful. Like rearranging the clouds."

Tony read the note, blinked, re-read it and then read it *again* in rising wonder. *Lena* had written this? He looked up quickly but of course she was nowhere to be seen. In fact she was back at her desk far across the office hunched over some papers, pretending to work, but really only cowering in angst-y anticipation of what he'd think and say about what she had written to him. Or *not* say which would be even worse.

Writing sexy notes to lovers was a breeze for Lena. She'd done it regularly in the past and the men loved them—yummy junk food for the mind; Doritos for the libido. But this note was dead-honest, like nothing she'd written before to any man she was involved with. It let her heart's guard down and told Tony Areal the truth about how she felt. That was awfully scary stuff. Especially for someone like Lena who could wrap most of Earth's male population around her finger simply by slinking into a room wearing too much eye shadow and attitude. Yet that morning while sitting on the toilet of all places, something in both her head and heart unexpectedly went *clunk*, like two railroad freight cars being joined together. Eyes wide with startled awe, Lena instantly knew that whatever fondness, fervor, or fuckiness she had previously felt for her new lover was way way back in her rearview mirror now and she realized for the first time she had crossed the border into a whole new state of mind re: Mr. Anthony Areal.

How *does* it happen? What is the tipping point from fond to fervor? Surprisingly often it can be as simple as a gesture, their hand dropped onto your knee while riding together in a train, or the way they so seriously but sloppily brush their teeth in the morning. A small detail, trivial, that blossoms in an instant into the most important thing in your life. That innocent hand on the knee sealed the deal. Our mistake is to think love makes sense when much of the time it is, for better or worse, the most irrational thing we experience. Sometimes the biggest loves rise out of the shadows of our emotions like ghosts right in our face, but instead of hooting *Boo!* they say *Now! Them!*

Sitting on the toilet that morning, the only thing Lena could think to say upon realizing she had fallen in love with Tony Areal was, "uh oh."

Sometime later she took the note she'd written and re-read four times out of the wastebasket where she'd tossed it. She fretted out loud, "Damn you—*give* it to him. It's nice. He'll like it." But what if he *didn't*? For Lena Schabort it was a large act of moxie and courage later that morning to actually drop the squashed ball of paper on his desk and hurry away so she didn't have to see him read it.

For the next awful hour Tony didn't respond. Not an email, not a note, a drive-by smile on his way to the office coffee machine—nada. She didn't even see him which was strange because their office wasn't that big. Oh God, was he avoiding her? Lena's inner weather roiled crazily in that hour. Maybe he read her note, thought it was sweet but nothing special. No response required. That made sense. She hadn't said anything especially mushy or over the top—sweetly romantic and a little poetic, right? So, no response=no problem.

But maybe he had read it and was *horrified* by what it said—"tender and wild and beautiful." Why had she used those loaded words when she could so easily have written something typical like, "Last night was so *hot* with you." And top off that mundanity with a silly photo of, like, a wolf howling at the moon.

Maybe his silence meant nothing...or everything. She was miserable.

Lena Schabort was not used to these kinds of feelings for a man, any man. In the past several had loved her, but she only liked or lusted them back—never more. Until she got involved with Tony she was fine with that. She liked being squired and admired, *really* liked sex, and one of the few rock solid beliefs she'd carried all through life was a genuine faith in the idea that one day she *would* meet a man she'd want to wake up next to for the rest of her life. Lena was not a religious person but believed that religiously. And she was willing to wait however long it took, not for some unrealistic Prince Charming or Mr. Right-movie star-zillionaire, but a man she could honestly say, "You are my home" to and mean it.

Another half hour passed and still no sign of him. By then, Lena had nervously drunk so much coffee her bladder was the size of a ripe coconut and warned if she didn't go to the bathroom soon she'd burst.

To her surprise as soon as she sat down on the toilet, her eyes teared up and she started to cry. Because she remembered the big revelation about her feelings for Tony occured on a toilet a few hours before. But now look what was happening—for the first time in her life she'd put a whole foot in the deep end of love's pool but from all (silent) indications, a shark was in the midst of biting it off.

When she finished peeing, she took a while in front of the bathroom mirror bringing her face back to a semblance of normal before going back out and confronting the office world again. Then, to add insult to injury, who should be perched on a corner of her desk looking smug as an African dictator but the horrible Rick Olivier. She was so disgusted he was there at a moment when her heart was a nervous wreck, that she felt like clonking him over the head with a wastebasket.

"What do you want Rick? Go away. You are the Ebola virus to me right now." She tried to vaporize him with a glare of pure loathing but as usual Godzilla-Ego heard only what he wanted to hear and ignored both her venomous look and the insult.

"Are you finally learning to cook, Lena? It's about time. But we should cook together sometime." He leered. "I told you before—If I cook you a meal it'll be so delicious you'll immediately want to elope with me, guaranteed. So let's have a cooking date—how does that sound?"

"What are you talking about?"

She hadn't noticed he had something in his hand. He held it up now and she saw what it was—a can opener. A simple metal can opener.

Eyes widening, Lena recognized it immediately and could barely believe what she was seeing. It couldn't be. But it was! *It was!* Her voice spilled out in a thrilled rush, *"Where did you get that?"*

Rick frowned. "It was here on your desk. Why?"

"Was there a note? Was there anything with it?"

Shaking his head, dismay slid down his face like a slow dropping curtain as this conversation went south in a way he hadn't expected. Lena snatched the metal opener out of his hand; *kissed* the damned thing, and without another word hurried away to who-knows-where.

Offended, Olivier stood up, shot his cuffs, and made sure no one else had seen Lena Schabort bound away from him like he had cooties. "Fuck her," he grumbled on his way back to his desk. Then sighing added mournfully, "You *wish, Amico,* you wish she'd let you in."

TEACHING THE DOG TO READ

TO LENA'S dismay, Tony wasn't at his desk when she got there, can opener in nervous hand. On the way there she'd rehearsed what to say and even slowed a few feet from his desk so as not to be winded and unable to speak the carefully chosen words when she arrived.

Her first thought had been to flat out ask him, "Does this mean what I think it means?" But she knew that could easily come across as too aggressive and besides, what if Tony *hadn't* put the thing on her desk—someone else had for some reason? Then she'd sound confusing and foolish, so scratch that line too. How about if she were to hold up the gadget and ask him, "Was this from you?" Simple, straightforward, with no hint of anything else behind the question. But again, if that can opener on her desk *wasn't* from Mr. Areal, the subject would end there and she'd be left with a useless piece of metal in her hand and a wincing heart.

What she finally settled on saying was the question, "Is this from Gorbog too?" and hope he'd remember what she was talking about.

A few nights before, Tony had a dramatic dream that he described to her as soon as they woke up the next morning. "We were in the kitchen making a meal together. I don't remember what it was, but that's not important." Lena wasn't fully awake while he spoke but the eager, urgent tone of his voice said the dream meant a lot to him so she should listen carefully.

"The front doorbell rang and I went to answer it. When I came back I was carrying a small box. The return address said only that it was from someone (?) named Gorbog."

Still sleepy-headed, Lena squinted at the wacky name, not sure she'd heard him right. *Who?*

"Gorbog. I have no idea who or what that is. When I opened the box, the only thing inside was a can opener. The basic kind with two wings joined at the center you hook onto the lip of a can, close them, and then turn the key to open it?" Tony put his hands together and opened/closed them in an upside down "V" to demonstrate the kind of opener he was describing.

Lena nodded she understood.

"I took it out of the box and suddenly this *light* went on in my head. I knew exactly what it was for and why it'd been sent to me." Tony sat up in bed and wiped his mouth. "I told you to take one side of it and I'd take the other. Then we were supposed to make a wish and pull it apart, like a regular wishbone on a chicken—"

Lena raised one eyebrow and closed the other eye. "Make a wish and pull a metal *can opener* apart?"

"Yes I know it sounds crazy, but let me finish—you're going to like this next part, believe me. So we made our wishes and on the count of three, pulled like you do on any wishbone. The thing broke apart, but in the exact middle so neither got the short end. Neither of us won or lost. The opener snapped *precisely* in half.

"You looked at me and asked what it meant. I said because we'd both made the same wish, now it was going to come true. You didn't believe me and asked what I'd wished for. I said that our relationship would last. You started crying because that *was* your wish too."

Hearing this, Lena jerked up onto her elbows and stared at Tony, her eyes full of hope, doubt and a million questions. She didn't know what to say while at the same time she was bursting to say so much.

There are moments in any relationship which can come at the beginning, middle or end, where everything balances on a single word or sentence. Even one look can sometimes steady, or knock everything of importance onto its side, never to be righted again. Lena Schabort, who wasn't often at a loss for words in her life, was terrified to say the wrong thing at this moment. Tony's dream was so exciting in what it might mean for her future that perhaps it was better to remain silent and let his strange beautiful story simply breathe itself into life between them now like a just-born child, rather than if she were to say something that might spoil its promise.

"It's...lovely, Tony; like a mysterious perfume you smell only once but then it's gone."

He smiled and looked down at his hands. Was he waiting for her to say more, to give a better (fuller, more coherent...) response that would seal their deal right there and then? Was recounting the dream his shy unique way of saying in real life his world was hers if she wanted it? Lena badly needed Tony to look up now so she could read his face for a sign. But to her dismay he said in a quieter subdued voice that he had to go to the toilet. Then to add to the disappointment he got out of bed and padded to the bathroom without looking back.

Fists clenched tight with frustration, Lena sat in the middle of the bed fretting about what she should/would/could have done or said to make things right. Her frustration got worse when she heard the shower go on in there, which meant he wouldn't be out of the bathroom for a while.

When he did emerge an eternity later he smiled, told her he had to go back to his place to pick up his laptop, and would see her at work. When she asked lamely while he was dressing if he wouldn't like some coffee first, the words were barely out of her mouth when she remembered he didn't drink coffee, which made her sound like a complete ditz.

TEACHING THE DOG TO READ

"Hey, I'm the tea guy, remember? I'll see you later."

LATER **SHE** stood by the side of his office desk holding a can opener in her hand wondering where the hell he was because if he didn't show up soon she felt she'd pop.

IT MUST have been something he ate. But he hadn't eaten anything since the night before and that was only a burger and fries—nothing special or especially volcanic to cause the disturbing hot solid tightness in the middle of his chest that blossomed as he was walking in to work. It sat stolidly there like a fat woman on a bus taking up most of the room on the seat. He'd had heartburn before but nothing like this.

Tony had lied to Lena earlier about needing his laptop. He left her apartment after showering so he could go to a hardware store and buy the can opener. Then get to the office and leave it on her desk before she arrived. He was able to do all that, but now this chest-thing became so dominant and worrying that he finally stood up and walked to the bathroom, hoping some physical movement would calm it or maybe even make it go away.

No luck. The fat woman inside his chest stayed right where she was. While washing his hands at the bathroom sink, he remembered the warning signs of a heart attack were exactly what were happening to him at that moment: tightness in the chest, a heat radiating up to below his chin, shortness of breath...

Uncle Bob. His Uncle Bob had died of a sudden heart attack. Oh God! Once that thought appeared he panicked. Without another word Tony Areal left the bathroom, left the office without a word to anyone, got in his car and drove fast to the hospital. He was terrified he'd die on the way over, minutes away from being saved. Please please, not that. Wait, I'm almost there. Please!

He didn't call Lena because on the drive over, the tightness in his chest increased and fear swallowed him. Not now! Not this! He was young, his health was good, and he had no real bad habits. All he could think about was sweet Uncle Bob and then dead Uncle Bob and he tried to breathe deep and normally but nothing did what he wanted. His breath came and went in short doggy pants. Then a thin wire of silvery pain slid down his left arm into his hand. He took that hand off the steering wheel and shaking it told it to wait, please wait till we get there.

TEACHING THE DOG TO READ

He made it to the hospital. Driving straight up to the ambulance entrance, he got out of the Porsche, waved at an orderly on the other side of the glass doors to come, and collapsed. By the time they got him on a stretcher and were racing him through hospital corridors while pounding him on the chest, Tony Areal had no pulse.

"WHAT THE hell did you *do*?"

"*Nothing*; I did nothing!"

"I warned you about the chest pains."

"You did not! I would have done something if I knew. Do you think I'm stupid? Do you think I want to die?"

"Looks like it's too late for that now."

Tony Night looked at Tony Day with disgust. "Why are you giving up so easily? You don't know if we're going to die. We've got things to live for. At least I do, I don't know about you."

The two Tonys sat in flimsy white plastic chairs on either side of the bed where the comatose body of their host Anthony Areal lay. The chairs were so low both men had to crane their necks to see over the body when they wanted to make eye contact with each other.

"So what the hell happened, you keeled over?"

"Yeah, as soon as I got out of the car it knocked me flat. Thank God I got as far as the hospital. What if I were still driving and crashed into something?"

"Yeah well, it looks like you *did* crash into something—death."

Annoyed, Tony Night shook his head. How was he supposed to have known about the bum heart? Tony Day had never brought anything about a bad heart into his dreams. And anyway, who dreams about having a heart condition?

"Who's that?"

Back to the door, Tony Day didn't know who Night was talking about. "Who's *who*?"

Tony Night gestured with his chin toward the door. "*Him.*"

Day turned halfway around in his chair. Standing a few feet away was one of the handsomest men he had ever seen. Movie star handsome with long black hair combed straight back, sharply chiseled features like a 1930's Fascist statue, and eyes that would make any soul sigh, male or female. The tall man was dressed in a gunmetal gray suit tailored so perfectly to his thin body that it looked like it had been poured onto him. In his hand he held a short fat lit cigar but strangely no smoke came from it, even when he took a puff and exhaled. The end glowed bright orange when he drew on the cigar but not one thread or curl of smoke came off it.

TEACHING THE DOG TO READ

The guy checked the time on his wristwatch. Tony Day recognized it immediately—a Lichtenberg 'Figure.' Instinctively Tony looked down at his wrist but his Lichtenberg was still there.

"Len Fischman."

"Excuse me?"

"My name is Len Fischman." Another puff on the cigar. Fischman squinted one eye almost closed, as if smoke had gotten into it. But there was no smoke.

"Who are you? I mean, besides Len Fischman?"

"Number 43 or 44, I'm not really sure which because I never checked. I didn't care, you know what I mean?"

The Tonys glanced at each other, as if one might know what this Len was talking about and could fill the other in.

"What is—" both of them spoke this at the same time. Tony Day shut up and let his counterpart finish the sentence.

Tony Night said, "What is 43 or 44?"

"Incarnation. I came right before you. Sometimes it happens immediately after someone dies, sometimes it can be millennia. You came immediately. Don't ask me why."

When neither Tony said anything and looked baffled by what he had said, Fischman continued with noticeable exasperation at their confusion.

"*Reincarnation*? Past lives? Come on boys, you can't be *that* dense."

Still the Tonys remained silent.

Fischman rolled his eyes, put the cigar out on the floor and slid both hands into his pockets. "When were you born?"

"March 7."

"What year?"

"1973."

"Exactly. Well, on *March 6, 1973* I was driving a brand new Porsche I had picked up at the factory in Stuttgart along the Dalmatian Coast with my fiancée Alice—"

"*Alice*, did you say?" Tony Day didn't like hearing that name of his dream woman coming from this Len Fischman.

"Yes Tony, *Alice*. We were supposed to get married in Dubrovnik the next week. We had spent a fine Spring afternoon drinking way too much of a tasty regional wine called *Grk* and were driving back to our hotel when a large orange truck coming towards us blew a tire and drove right into us. Boys, the next day you were born. Now do you *capite*?"

"I'm you, reincarnated?" Tony Day asked incredulously.

"That is correct. And that is why you have been dreaming about a lovely woman named Alice."

TEACHING THE DOG TO READ

"Why are you here?" Tony Night asked. Tony Day was too stunned to say anything.

"To accompany you over to the other side. It's a nice system— Whoever preceded you comes back to guide you." Fischman smirked at the joke he was about to make. "Anyway, you'd have a hard time understanding Gorbog if he came for you."

Both Tonys remembered the strange name—it was written on the box that held the can opener in Tony Night's dream.

"Who is Gorbog?"

"The great granddaddy of us all, brother—the first in our blood line. 27,000 years ago Gorbog was born in what is now Russia. You'll meet him eventually. By then, after you've acclimated, you'll understand him. He's actually quite chatty. "

"But I don't *want* to die. I'm not ready." Tony Day wailed.

"Me neither," Tony Night agreed, shooting a hurt look over at Tony Day for not having said 'we' don't want to die.

"Boys, I didn't either; I was about to get married. But it's out of your hands." Fischman pointed to the body lying on the bed. "Once the motor conks out, that's the end of you."

"Is it going to happen soon?"

"I dunno. That's always up to your body. I'm just here to introduce myself. Normally I wouldn't show up until after you died, but because you guys traded places they sent me across a little earlier than usual."

"Across?"

Fischman looked from side to side as if to make sure no one could hear what he was about to say to the Tonys. "I'm not supposed to tell you this till it's over, but the Afterlife? It's over there. Two steps away." He hooked a thumb out to the side like a hitchhiker trying to catch a ride. "You wanna take a little look at your new home?"

"No!" both Tonys shouted.

Fischman held up both hands, palms out in surrender. "Okay, okay I was only trying to make it easier for you when the time comes. It's really nice over there, believe me. I didn't even want to come over here now and leave it."

"No!" The Tonys said again, even more adamantly.

The door crept slowly open and Lena Schabort entered.

Eyebrows raised, Len Fischman checked her out from top to bottom and gave an exaggerated approving nod. When she saw the body of Anthony Areal on the bed, she quickly covered her mouth with both hands and began to weep. Lena tried to muffle the noise with her hands by pressing harder against her mouth but that only made new louder sounds. She stood there unmoving, paralyzed by what she was seeing.

Tony Night got up from his chair and was going to go to her, but Fischman shook his head. "You're in a coma. She can't see either of you. Only the Tony she knew, and that's old dead weight over there."

When she was able to calm down a little and gather herself, Lena walked to the side of the bed and looked down at her new love. Hesitantly, she touched his right hand with her index finger but for seconds, as if afraid even one touch might worsen his condition. Then she did something else that made all three men in the room catch their breath.

Bending over the still body, she stretched her arms out and without touching Tony, put her hands near either side of his face, as if cradling it. Leaning forward, she lowered her forehead until it almost touched his. She stayed in that reverent position for a long time.

Both Tony Day and Len Fischman eventually looked at Tony Night with great sympathy and a little jealousy in their eyes. It was so plain this woman was crazy about the Tony Areal she knew and her grief was palpable. It was clear that when he died she would be crushed.

To make matters worse, outside on the street a cacophony of auto horns went by and from their cheerful, uneven rhythm it sounded like either a wedding party celebrating, or some sports team had won a game and this was a spontaneous victory parade announcing to the world the good news.

When Lena finally drew her hands back and lifted her head, she sat down in one of the chairs next to Tony's bed.

"You don't have to see this if you don't want."

"What?" Tony Night had been so absorbed watching Lena's every move that he'd barely heard Fischman speak.

"You don't have to watch this. You're in a coma. Both of you can go back into it. I don't know what's going on in his head now, but probably nothing. His brain is probably blank and biding its time till the body's clock runs down. You don't have to see this if you don't want. I wouldn't."

The Tonys looked at each other but neither had an answer.

"If it makes your decision any easier, you can come out again whenever you want. So long as the body is still alive, you—"

"—can come out again. Yeah, we heard you," Tony Day cut in. He looked at Night who, absolutely bereft, kept staring at Lena. Day knew it was his call and looking at Fischman, barely nodded his assent. All three men disappeared.

A few moments after they were gone Lena took a cell phone out of her purse and called a number on the phone's speed dial. The whole time she waited for it to connect, she stared at Tony and kept wiping her eyes with her free hand.

Her head snapped up when the other person answered. She said only, "I need your help," then paused and sucked in her lower lip while listening to the answer. She nodded assertively at something that was said. "Yes. Yes, I'm sure. I wouldn't ask for your help if I wasn't sure. He *is* the one but there's a problem now. Only you can help me." She listened and kept nodding at what she heard.

A minute later she disconnected the phone without saying anything more. Dropping it back into her purse she reached in for something else: a pad of paper and a black roller ball pen. She put the purse on the floor next to her chair, the pad and pen in her lap. She looked at Tony. She wasn't ready to begin yet and needed to see him before she did. Twice Lena picked up the pad only to put it down again. She dropped her chin to her chest and closed her eyes. An idea came and she smiled for the first time since hearing the bad news about him earlier at work. Picking up her purse she rummaged around inside it until she found the can opener he'd left on her desk what seemed like a long time ago. Taking hold of both sides of the tool, she opened and closed them several times. Once she held it up as if to show him what she was doing—open closed open closed… As if he could see. If only he *could* see now.

"I love this thing so much, Tony. You have no idea what it means to me."

She put the opener back in her purse, zipped it closed, took a deep breath and picking up the pen and pad, began to draw.

One look at her work was all that was needed to tell Lena Schabort was a terrible artist. She drew a head as round as a balloon that looked like something a young child would draw. She put ears on this 'head' that looked like handles on a teacup rather than human ears. The eyes she drew were ridiculous, as was the nose and mouth. Again, when she finished the sketch it resembled something a six or seven year old might draw in kindergarten with a thick crayon.

A nurse came into the room, checked the chart at the foot of the bed and the glowing yellow numbers on the complicated looking machine Tony was connected to via multiple wires. Lena asked if there had been any change in his condition since he was admitted. The nurse gave a small tight smile and said she didn't think so, but Lena should ask the doctor when she made her rounds in the next half hour. Lena thanked her and said she would.

After the nurse left Lena tore the sketch out of the notebook, dropped it into her purse and began another. By the time the doctor arrived almost an hour later, she had completed seven and was working on an eighth. The difference between her first drawing and the latest one was astounding. If the first looked like the work of an untalented child, the eighth looked like the highly polished and professional product of a very good street portrait artist. Anyone who knew Tony and saw this drawing would have immediately said it was him to a tee. What's more, it was a portrait that caught something ineffable and strikingly intimate about him despite the fact it was a simple black and white drawing.

The emergency room doctor entered Anthony Areal's room with the pompous, *l'etat c'est moi*-drama of a famous opera star making her first appearance on stage to a richly-deserved ovation at the beginning of a performance. Doctor Mukherjee was good at her job but nowhere near *as* good as she thought she was. Privately the nurses called her "Dr. Legend" as in 'she's a legend in her own mind.'

When she saw the woman sitting by the side of the patient's bed drawing, the doctor did an instant assessment of her (face, hair, clothes, purse...) and then mentally chose which of her professional personas to present—firm but pleasant with a soupcon of professional know-it-all arrogance thrown in. "I'm Doctor Mukherjee," she said in an assertive voice while looking at the clipboard she carried, as if searching for some detail there. "And you are?"

"Lena Schabort. I'm his fiancée."

"I see." The doctor slid a pair of thick blue eyeglasses out of her left breast pocket and put them on. Taking the chart off the hook at the foot of the patient's bed, she examined the information there while carefully keeping her face blank. Then she looked at the numbers on the machine next to the bed and wrote several things on the chart. After a while it was only pretense because she was really only waiting for Lena to bombard her with questions which was what loved ones of the critically ill almost always did. Was there hope? Would they survive? Could anything more be done? Can they hear us? Do they know we're here? Dr. Rani Mukherjee had heard all these questions so many times over the years in voices that ranged from the petrified to the outraged. As a result she had developed a litany of automatic, highly technical responses that in most cases calmed but did not specifically encourage the questioners. She did not believe in creating false hope.

From the information on this man's chart, things did not look good for him and she was prepared to say exactly that if his fiancée wanted to know the truth. If the woman asked if he would recover, the doctor would say something along the lines of it's too soon to tell— What's happened to him is *extremely* serious and though he's stable for now, there's little else we can do until—

"Doctor?"

Here it comes.

"Yes?"

"Are you her?"

Certainly not expecting *this*, the doctor paused and frowned. "Excuse me?"

"Are you her?"

"I'm sorry. I don't understand."

Instead of clarifying the question, Lena held up her latest drawing of Tony. Doctor Mukherjee looked at it, saw it was done with great skill and was obviously of the patient, but beyond that she had no idea what this woman was talking about. Was she acting this oddly out of grief? Or perhaps she had gone quietly mad because of her fiancée's dire condition. Or maybe was she a plain old weirdo.

To the doctor's growing dismay, Lena repeated the gnomic question and added another, "Are you *her*? Is this drawing enough?"

On new unsure ground now the doctor asked carefully, "Would you like something to calm you down? We can arrange for—"

Lena said no and put the drawing back in her lap. "I'm fine. I thought you were someone else. Sorry if I confused you."

"You're sure you wouldn't like something—"

"No Doctor, really—I'm good."

"Do you have any questions?"

"No."

"*None*? No concerns about—"

Lena looked disinterested, as if the conversation was already over and she was being nice answering the question. "Nope, I'm fine. I'll sit here and keep him company."

Now it was the doctor who spoke uncertainly. "All right. But if you *do* want anything, the nurse's station is down the hall."

"Thank you. I'm sure I'll be fine."

Dr. Mukherjee was glad to get out of there but on her way down the hall she stopped one of the duty nurses and told her to keep an eye on the woman in 17 because she might be a little...*off*. The nurse said she would and the doctor continued on her rounds.

＝＊＝

TWO HOURS later Lena went down to the snack bar in the hospital lobby for an egg salad sandwich and bottle of mineral water. Opening the door to Tony's room again with food in hand, she was jolted to see a heavyset man sitting in her chair by the side of the bed. His large head was covered with the transparent reddish fuzz of a short crew cut, small ears, big mouth and wide nose… On first glance he reminded her of a professional wrestler or night club bouncer. Thick hands folded peacefully in his lap, his eyes were closed when she first entered. They opened when she cleared her throat and they were surprisingly gentle looking. He wore a crisp looking cobalt blue work shirt with the name DAVE in black letters on a white patch over his left breast.

"Lena?"

"Yes."

"I'm Dave. Do you have the drawings?"

Startled because she had been expecting a woman, Lena hesitated. "*You're* here for them? I thought—"

"I know what you're thinking, but I am the one. Can I see them please?"

"Yes, of course." She opened her purse and took out the now twelve portraits of Tony Areal she had drawn. She walked over to Dave and handed them to him. He studied each carefully for a long time, returning to several again and again. Others he barely glanced at. Surprisingly those were her later drawings that displayed the talent and finesse of a real professional artist. But Dave didn't appear interested in a finished product.

Lena stood by nervously, not knowing what to think or do. Finally he took so long reviewing them that she sat down in the chair on the other side of the bed and began eating her sandwich.

In time he brought the sheaf of sketches to his chest and shook his head. "No."

"*No?*"

"No. It's not there yet." He patted his chest with the papers. "One or two of them come close, but none captures exactly how you feel about him. Without that, we can't do anything. You'll have to keep at it." His voice was kind and even a little mournful but clearly not to be challenged. The answer was no and that ended the discussion.

The two of them sat in silence for a while.

"Are you going to finish that sandwich?"

She looked at it in her hand. "Uh no—would you like it?"

"I would. It looks good."

She walked the rest of her sandwich over to the other side of the bed and handed it to Dave. In exchange, he gave her the drawings. She went back to her chair and looked at them while he slowly and with obvious relish ate what was left of her egg salad.

Raising her head from the failed drawings, Lena had to know. "Can I ask you something?"

"Sure." Dave took an ironed white handkerchief out of a pocket and wiped the corners of his mouth.

"What did I do wrong here? How do I get it right?" Lena heard the strain in her voice, almost a whine, and didn't like it. To her it was a sign of weakness when she needed to be strong and sharp. But she also knew this was her one big chance and if she blew it, there wouldn't be another. Ever.

"There's no *you* in any of those drawings, Lena." Dave ate the last bit of sandwich, chewed a long time and swallowed. "You're trying so hard to draw him exactly that you're forgetting *you're* creating the picture. You must find a way to include your feelings and vision into the work for it to be complete. You really love this man? I don't see that here. Love, desire, all the things that attract you to him... None of it's here—only a few nice portraits.

"So far what you've done is rendered with a camera's eye some man—some *guy*. Like you drew a bunch of pictures of a stranger you passed on the street. In all of them except a few sections of the early ones where you were drawing like the girl you once were, it feels like you're consciously trying to erase any trace of yourself from the work. Don't do that, Lena—do the *opposite*."

Dave stood up, brushed a few bread crumbs off the front of his shirt and made for the door. But once there he stopped abruptly, walked back to her and asked for the drawings. Timidly she held them out. He shuffled through the pile until he came to the last, most accomplished one she'd done. Taking a fluorescent orange SHARPIE felt tip marker out of a pocket, he uncapped it and wrote something across the middle of the drawing, ruining it. Capping the marker, he handed the papers back to her and said, "Show me *that*." Then he left the room. On the drawing he had written inside a large orange heart:

LENA LOVES TONY. WHY?

WHEN DR. Mukherjee entered the room again several hours later it was because she had been called there by one of the duty nurses. These women had seen pretty much everything in their years working on the emergency ward but still now and then something extraordinary happened there that had them all buzzing. This time while walking quickly together down the hall to room 17, the nurse would say only that the doctor had to see this to believe it. Mukherjee didn't like that kind of unprofessional blurry talk, but kept her mouth shut. She knew she was unpopular among the nursing staff. As a result, they were always looking for things to add to their "Dr. Legend the Loser" list. Yes, Mukherjee knew all about her nickname and that list because she had her spies. Oh yes, she most certainly had her spies. But the doctor chose to ignore both for now and get on with her duties.

TEACHING THE DOG TO READ

The first thing she saw in room 17 when the nurse opened the door was the can opener. An everyday can opener sat on the patient's bedside table for some reason. More improbably Anthony Areal, who gave every physical indication he would die the last time the doctor saw him, was sitting up in that bed with a big smile on his face while holding hands with the woman who'd been in there earlier.

"What's happened here?"

Lena said, "He woke up a while ago and we've been sitting here talking since then."

Mukherjee glanced over at the nurse but the woman only shrugged and nodded agreement to what the fiancée had said. When the doctor looked away, the nurse made eye contact with Lena and gave her a big wink. She thought what had happened was miraculous and wonderful.

In contrast, Dr. Mukherjee did *not* like miracles. She liked facts, logic, things that made sense and all things teleological. That was one of the main reasons why she had gone into medicine. These kinds of inexplicable anomalies in her practice disturbed her greatly because they ran counter to everything she believed and wanted to believe about life and her life's work. When 2&2 didn't equal 4 in her day, no matter what the reason, some part of her very adept brain stopped, then started to burn and melt like film in a broken projector.

"Where is his chart?"

The nurse handed it over and stood back. She'd seen *that* look on the doctor's face before and knew it could well lead to bitchy or nasty. Tony and Lena ignored both women and looked tenderly at each other, or now and then at their talismanic can opener.

The doctor reviewed all the numbers and notations on Anthony Areal's chart but still disbelieving, did it again even more slowly. From all indications, this man should have been a goner.

"How do you feel?"

"Fine. Good. Like I woke up from a nap."

"A *nap*?" However professional she was normally, Mukherjee couldn't keep the incredulity out of her voice.

"Yeah, exactly like that—a nap." He looked again at his fiancée who radiated happiness.

"I need to speak with the original attending physician. I'll be back." The doctor turned on her heel and left the room, followed shortly by the nurse who couldn't resist giving Lena another happy wink before she went away. Whether Tony's lightning fast recovery was a miracle or not, the nurses on the emergency ward were always delighted when unexpected happy endings like this occurred in their otherwise sad outpost.

Mukherjee needed a place to talk to Tony's doctor in private and ask certain vital questions. She knew the nurses wanted to hear the conversation, so she decided to go all the way back to her office to make the call in private, away from snooping ears.

"Who's that?"

"One of my doctors. I remember her voice. I didn't see her but that Indian accent…"

Although no one could see them, four men sat outside room 17 in the hospital hallway on chairs facing each other. Tony Day and Night on one side, Len Fischman and Gorbog on the other. Gorbog was naked except for a filthy tattered loincloth and a seriously hirsute body and head. When he stood he wasn't tall but if you told people he was a yeti, many would believe you by the look of him. He spoke in a definite language but to the two Tonys it only sounded like a variety of different toned guttural grunts. Fischman had to translate everything he said, not that it was much.

"What did she *do*? Why are we here? Will someone please tell me what happened to me? To *us*?" Tony Day looked at his other self, ashamed for not having included him.

Gorbog made a stern face and punched Fischman on the arm, wanting to know what the hairless one had said. Gorbog knew who Tony Day was but didn't like what he saw of his future self. He didn't like Fischman either but at least *that* hairless one could speak his language. Len translated what

Tony had said and the caveman grumpily grunted his agreement. All four men wanted to know what had happened half an hour before. Why was some alien, not quite right version of themselves sitting comfortably and in love with Lena Schabort in the other room while the real thems sat out here in the hall scratching their heads.

No one said anything for a while. They all sat there looking glum and confused while they watched nurses and patients pass by. Of course none of the people could see these four. The two Tonys didn't understand it either because unlike Gorbog and Len Fischman, they weren't dead. Proof of that was a few feet away in room 17 where some *new* version of Anthony Areal was alive and being adored by a desirable woman. None of this made sense but that's what happens when from one minute to the next you're sort of not here anymore.

The door at the end of the long hall opened and a big husky man with short reddish hair came moseying down towards them. He carried a large plastic bag in one hand. He wore a blue shirt with DAVE written on a patch over his breast. Tony Day thought he must be one of the hospital workers until the man came right over and sat next to Gorbog.

"What's up, fellas? Anyone here hungry? I am."

The four men, by now used to being invisible to the hospital's passing parade, looked at each other. This guy *sees* us?

Dave opened the bag and peered inside. "I've got two pastramis with coleslaw and Russian dressing for the Tonys, a Reuben for me, and a meatball sub for Len. That's your favorite, right?" Turning to Gorbog, he spoke a few guttural grunts the yeti seemed to understand. "Okay then, let's hit it." Dave passed around the sandwiches and lastly took out a large hunk of what appeared to be scorched-black meat. Gorbog snatched it from him and buried his mouth in it. The other three men held the sandwiches in their hands and watched their ancestor noisily devour a lump of twenty thousand year old burnt something.

While eating, all of them kept looking at Dave to see if he was going to say anything. But he seemed content to silently devour his jumbo Reuben sandwich and stare at his feet while chewing. Dave considered eating a form of meditation and if it had been up to him, he would have eaten all of his meals alone. But that's not how it worked with this job.

One Tony turned to the other and said in frustration under his breath, "This is *fucked up*."

"The sandwich?"

"No—this situation!"

That got Dave's attention. He sighed, knowing he had to talk now. "When she was eighteen, Lena tried to kill herself. She should have died but Alice didn't want that to happen so she saved her."

"Alice?" Tony Day interrupted. That name at this moment was like an electric shock to him.

Dave nodded, then said be quiet and listen. "When Lena recovered, Alice asked why she did it? The girl said she was lonely and afraid she'd never find a man who really loved her and wanted to be with her forever. So Alice being Alice made the girl an offer: whenever Lena found *the* man she believed was the love of her life, she was to call a special telephone number Alice gave her. Only once in her life could she make the call, so she'd better be sure of her choice. Because if she chose wrong, she would be cursed with this man's company for all of her lives to come. Lena chose you, Tony."

Tony Night sat up straighter in his chair, pleased and proud, while at the same time he got the feeling there was more to this story and from Dave's tone of voice, it wasn't all good.

"When she finally made that call, Alice told her to draw a portrait of you from her heart and soul. If she did it right, that would seal you two together forever. If she thought you were perfect as you were, then she was to draw *that* Tony. But if there were things she wanted changed about you or your personality, little adjustments here and there, she was to include those too.

"She had to draw as many pictures as was necessary to capture her essential vision of you, and Alice said it might take her a long time. But it didn't, as you can see. Lena's heart knew exactly the Anthony Areal she wanted and that's the version of you alive in the other room now."

Almost as soon as Dave finished speaking, Gorbog disappeared.

Dave glanced to where the man had been sitting but then went back to eating. The others stared fearfully at Gorbog's empty chair and at Big Dave enjoying his sandwich.

"What the hell was *that*? Where did he go?" The last bit of meat Gorbog was eating had dropped to the floor when he evaporated. Len Fischman pointed to it with his foot.

Dave said, "He's not part of the Anthony Areal Lena wants in her life so he's no longer needed.

"Sorry to say neither are you, Leonard; she doesn't like sleazy guys. But without you Mr. Lady's Man and your vast knowledge of women *somewhere* in his genes, Tony here would never have succeeded with Lena. That whole bit when he asked her to go dancing on their first date? Genius! All that was pure Leonard Fischman. So that's your legacy and you should be proud of it. But I would suggest finishing your sandwich soon because I don't know how long you've got." Dave turned to the Tonys. "You two guys are safe because you're obviously an integral part of the Anthony Areal she loves. But you're her base model Tony—like when you buy a new car? The final Tony Areal she drew began with you two, but then she added all kinds of extras she wanted in her partner. It will be interesting to see how that works out."

Dave chuckled in admiration. "Alice and her experiments. For as long as I've worked for her I never cease to be amazed at both her imagination and willingness to try different things. She's like a master chef in a great restaurant—always experimenting, always combining strange and even impossible things to see how they'll work together. She's indefatigable. She let you guys trade places like you did. That's never been done before. She let a once-suicidal woman *draw* her perfect partner... You should see that final drawing Lena did—it's as far from realism as you can imagine. I was shocked by it, but Alice wasn't. And the wonderful thing is she has no idea how these experiments will work out. Alice never interferes once she's set things in motion. You and Lena meeting and hooking up? Alice had nothing to do with that."

Len Fischman asked angrily, "Did she have anything to do with killing us? Did she crash that truck into us that day?"

"No, that's not how she works. The driver of that truck should have had the brakes inspected months before the accident but he was poor and couldn't afford any kind of repair so he kept putting it off."

Tony Day couldn't help asking, "Are we talking about the Alice from my dream?"

A chilling thought came to Len Fischman, "Or my *fiancée* Alice?"

"No boys, she's neither. The Alice I work for has fun sometimes inserting little bits of herself into peoples' lives and dreams to see how it will affect them. That's one of the reasons why you both fell in love with your women. Even old Gorbog had an Alice."

Tony Night was furious. Angry as all hell he stood up, threw what was left of his sandwich on the floor, marched right over to Dave in his chair and pointed a quivering finger at him. "Then what *does* happen to us now, *Dave? Sooner or later do we go up in smoke too like the caveman or him?"

Dave stared at Tony's discarded sandwich a few moments. "No. You two just now became part of their dreams. You'll come and go in the stories they tell themselves in their sleep for as long as they both live. It's a kind of immortality—in their dreams you'll never age beyond today."

There was a pause when the two Tonys looked at each other to see their reactions to what had been said. Finally one said to the other, "I *don't* think this is the beginning of a beautiful friendship, Louie."

BACK IN room 17, Tony Areal had fallen asleep holding Lena's hand. She was perfectly content to sit there and watch him, safe in the knowledge that soon enough he would wake and be back in her world again, in *their* world now, where all good things were possible and she would do everything in her power to be a worthy mate for him.

His eyes began to twitch and she could see his eyeballs move around beneath the lids. Tony was dreaming. Lena remembered his dream about the can opener and how such a silly little object changed the course of both their lives. She smiled thinking maybe he's having another can opener dream. Or maybe he's dreaming about us together somewhere wonderful.